P9-CKU-963

My

n

Book

by Jane Belk Moncure

illustrated by Linda Hohag

THE CHILD'S WORLD

ELGIN, ILLINOIS 60120

Library of Congress Cataloging in Publication Data

Moncure, Jane Belk.
  My "n" book.

  (My first steps to reading)
  Rev. ed. of: My n sound box. © 1979.
  Summary: Little n fills her box with many things
that begin with the letter "n."
  1. Children's stories, American. [1. Alphabet]
I. Hohag, Linda. ill. II. Moncure, Jane Belk.   My n
sound box.   III. Title.   IV. Series: Moncure, Jane Belk.
My first steps to reading.
PZ7.M739Myn   1984   [E]   84-17537
ISBN 0-89565-287-0

Distributed by Childrens Press, 1224 West Van Buren Street,
Chicago, Illinois 60607.

© 1984 The Child's World, Inc.
All rights reserved. Printed in U.S.A.
Special Revised Edition.

My "n" Book

Little  n had a  box.

She said, "I will fill my  box."

She found
nuts on a
nut tree.

Little  climbed the nut tree.

"I will pick nuts,"
she said.

Little  picked nine nuts.

She made the number 9.

Guess where she put the nine nuts and the number nine?

box

Little n picked more nuts.

She made nine sets of nuts.

Then Little n counted ninety nuts. She made the number 90.

She put all the
nuts into
her box.

box

Little n had ninety-nine nuts.

She made
the number 99.

Little n climbed the nut tree
again.

Little **n** saw

nightingales,

nine nightingales,
eating nuts.

The nightingales

had nests.

Little  put the nightingales and the nests into her box, carefully.

There were eggs in the nests.

Little **n** could not count
how many eggs.

Little  was sleepy. So she took...

...a nap.

The next day, Little 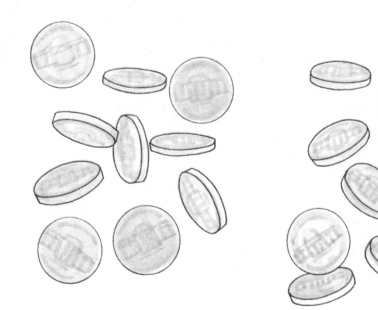 found nickels,
lots of nickels.

She counted

99 nickels.

Little  took her nickels to a store. She bought a necklace for mother, a necktie and a nutcracker for father.

Little **n** had 19 nickels left.

So she bought a nightgown for herself.

Little **n** took all her new things home. She put on her

nightgown.

Then she heard a noise.
Guess what? There were
baby nightingales
in the nests,
crying
for nuts.

box

"Don't cry,"
said Little n.

"I have nuts
for all of you."

nightingales

nests

nuts